My Good Neighbor

Extremely, Forced, Alpha, Monster, Cuckold, BDSM,

Poetic, Domination, Interracial, Dark Fantasy Story

Lana Kendra

it wasn't bought for your personal use only, go back to your favorite ebook retailer and buy your copy. Thank you for acknowledging this author's efforts.

Table of Contents

Content Warning

Due to its sexual content, this book is only for those over the age of legal adulthood. There are some topics with a lot of foul language. All of the characters are at least eighteen years old.

Introduction

Are you in search of an exciting and thrilling book to read? Look no further than this extensive collection of Erotic Suspense book. I offer a wide range of genres, including Romantic Erotica, Fantasy, and Urban BDSM Fiction, to cater to even the most discerning reader. Whether you enjoy Anthologies, Westerns, or Paranormal Romance, I have something to suit your taste. My collection also includes Poetic Folklore, Interracial, Black & African American Literary Criticism, and Gothic Horror for those who crave a deeper and darker reading experience. If you're interested in Futuristic, LGBTQ+, Short Stories, or Lesbian literature, my diverse range of options will keep you captivated. Additionally, I offer Humorous, Victorian, New Adult, and College Women's Psychological Mysteries for those seeking a lighter but equally engaging read. Furthermore, My Fairy Tale Collections,

Transgender, Contemporary Western, Bisexual, and Poetry genres will transport you to different worlds and explore a variety of themes. For my Teen and Young Adult readers, I have a selection of European Geography, Cultures, eBooks, Loners, Outcasts, Mythology, Folk Tales, and much more. With such a wide array of options to choose from, you'll never run out of thrilling and enchanting stories to immerse yourself in.

It is important to emphasize that this content is exclusively intended for individuals who are 18 years of age or older.

My Good Neighbor

The phone rang as Chaya was wrapping up the editing of her most recent fitness video. She glanced over and was shocked to find it was Avi, her neighbor. That is strange, she thought. Her next-door neighbor must have had a solid reason to call her out of the blue, since it was improper for males, especially married men, to phone women just to speak in their Ultra-Orthodox circles.

"Hi Ms. Goldstein, This is your neighbor Mr. Shapiro calling"

Although they both knew each other by their first name, Chaya couldn't help but find it amusing that he was using her last name in their small town, even though his voice was kind and welcoming. "Hello, Mr. Shapiro. How may I help you?"

Avi paused before adding, "Well, I typically wouldn't bother you about this, but my usual babysitter canceled and I just can't find a replacement. I usually wouldn't bother you but would it be ok for me to ask you to come by for an hour or so?"

Chaya's heart began to speed. Being a good neighbor meant lending a helping hand to those in need, and she felt very at ease looking after kids. Naturally, Mr. Shapiro.

Chaya answered, packing her laptop and grabbing her purse as she went—not forgetting to give herself a quick sniff of her favorite perfume—and headed toward the Shapiro mansion, sending a mist of sandalwood and jasmine behind her.

Chaya heard the enthusiastic babble of small children coming from upstairs as she entered the house and smiled to herself, remembering how much she liked being around children and how they always brought such joy and innocence into her life.

As Chaya slid onto the couch, Avi remarked, "They should

be 99% asleep by now. Thank you so much for stepping in."

"Not a problem at all," Chaya answered as the door shut behind him.

Chaya took out the book she carried with her and began to read.

Words blurred together on the page as her mind wandered back to the day Avi and his family had moved in; Chaya had been so concentrated on her own life that she hadn't given them much attention at first.

She recalled how she used to see Avi and his wife strolling together, smiling, talking animatedly—they appeared like the ideal couple—and then all of a sudden, out of the blue, they parted ways, with rumors circulating around their town about potential causes but no hard evidence ever coming to light.

Though Chaya didn't want to seem nosy, she couldn't help

but notice how successfully Avi adjusted to his new job as a single father: he made sure his kids were fed, washed, and entertained, and he even found time for exercise and housekeeping.

Chaya was in awe of Avi's strength and fortitude as she observed him interact with his kids. Despite all of the obstacles he had to overcome, he managed to handle everything with a grace and ease, and he looked amazing doing it. Chaya found it difficult to take her eyes off of Avi's broad shoulders, toned arms, and defined abs when he was swimming with his kids in their backyard pool.

She made an effort to concentrate on her reading, but her thoughts kept returning to the picture of Avi without a shirt, water cascading down his toned frame.

Chaya couldn't believe she was thinking like this about her neighbor, who was still legally married, and she felt bad for even thinking such thoughts, but she couldn't deny the strength of her desire. The more she thought about it, the more aroused she grew.

She saw herself and Avi playing tag in the pool, laughing so hard that their bodies collided, his powerful hands grabbing her waist as they raced across the water, their faces near enough to exchange gasps for breath.

Her pulse quickened, and she had a sudden craving to examine her own body. She reached under her dress and started to touch herself, running her fingers over her smooth skin, her breath getting harder as she touched, her desire growing.

She closed her eyes, engrossed in the sensation, her body vibrating with anticipation as she caressed herself, almost sensing Avi's hands on her, his lips caressing hers.

She heard footsteps suddenly approaching the room, immediately straightened her skirt, and looked up to see one of Avi's sons wiping his sleepy eyes in the doorway.

"Where's my daddy?"I asked.

"It's alright, my love. Chaya comforted him, hoping her voice would stay calm, "Your daddy will be here soon." The child nodded, yawning widely as he staggered back to his room.

Following him, Chaya made sure he was securely nestled under the covers. As she felt a wave of peace wash over her, she chose to read her book on the edge of the boy's bed until Avi came back. She was tired from her day, and the plush mattress felt good to lay on.

Her eyelids slowly started to droop as she read, and the peaceful ambiance and the rhythmic phrases lulled her into a deep state of relaxation. Before she knew it, Chaya was fast asleep, with her head propped up against the cushion.

Arriving home in silence, careful not to wake his sleeping kids, Avi was surprised to find Chaya nowhere to be found in the living room. Timidly tiptoeing by his son's bedroom, he couldn't help but observe Chaya curled up blissfully on his son's pillow.

He took a minute to observe her beauty as her long brown hair flowed over the pillow and her compassionate expression on her face conveyed the kindness that was in her heart.

Something about Chaya was just so remarkable that Avi experienced a rush of emotion that he had never imagined to feel about another lady.

While he watched her sleep, a range of feelings raced through Avi, including admiration for her generosity, brilliance, and beauty, as well as the fact that she had come through for him just when he needed it.

The sentiments were too strong to suppress, even though he knew he shouldn't be thinking about her in this way.

A few minutes of observing the calm rise and fall of her chest later, he called her name gently enough that Chaya's eyes fluttered open and she turned to stare up at him with a mixture of astonishment and shame.

Mr. Shapiro, oh! Chaya quickly got up, smoothed her hair, and apologized, saying, "I didn't mean to fall asleep."

With a smile that made his eyes wrinkle at the corners, Avi said, "Ms. Goldstein, don't worry about it. I recognize. You've been really beneficial today.

Chaya experienced an overwhelming sense of thankfulness. "Mr. Shapiro, thank you. I am grateful for the chance to assist. By the way, Ms. Goldstein sounds like I'm your teacher or something, so feel free to call me Chaya."

"Sure thing Chaya" , Avi replied. "And you can drop the title and call me Avi too."

Still blushing from being discovered asleep, Chaya decided to try and divert the subject by asking Avi about the framed photo of him going up a mountain that she observed on the wall.

"Wow, that is one amazing photo!Pointing at the picture, Chaya screamed, "Where did you take that?"

With pride, Avi recalled the moment, grinning, "It was taken on a trek in the Swiss Alps. It was an incredible encounter."

Excitement flashed in Chaya's eyes. "Switzerland Alps? That sounds amazing!

Avi arched an eyebrow, perplexed by her sudden shift of subject. "Oh, yes. That was quite an adventure."

Chaya grinned, happy to talk about something she was passionate about. "I'm an avid hiker myself, and I see that you've been to some pretty amazing places."

Are you free to talk about that?"Seems like you have some interesting stories yourself," Avi said, pointing to the kitchen. "Chaya agreed," she said, trailing behind him into the kitchen.

"So, what kinds of workouts are you into?Sincere in his curiosity regarding her hobbies, Avi enquired.

With joy lighting up her eyes, Chaya answered, "I love running, hiking, and swimming. I find that these activities help me stay both physically and mentally fit."

Avi smiled, appreciating her excitement "I've had the good fortune to visit and discover a lot of the world. And what's this? I've also found that, despite everything going on, maintaining my physical health and activity level keeps me centered and grounded."

"Exactly, it's not just about physical fitness; it's also about mental wellbeing." Chaya shouted.

Avi nodded, acknowledging her viewpoint and saying, "I totally agree. Nothing relieves stress and helps you decompress more than a vigorous workout."

Avi couldn't help but notice how gorgeous Chaya was, her dark brown hair framing her face and her eyes sparkling with warmth and intelligence as they talked about their favorite hikes, trails, and destinations. Their conversation flowed easily between personal experiences and common interests.

"You know Chaya, you look really good," Avi added in a lighthearted and humorous way. Avi couldn't resist complimenting Chaya.

Startled by his remark, Chaya flushed. "Thank you, Mr. Shapiro," she said, her cheeks getting redder.

"Oh my god, I can't believe it's already two in the morning. Look at the time!"Speaking, Chaya got up from her chair and moved in the direction of the front entrance.

Feeling guilty for keeping her up so late, Avi replied, "Sorry for keeping you up this late, Chaya."

"Oh, it's all right, Avi," Chaya answered. "I really enjoyed our talk!

"You too, Chaya."

Chaya couldn't help but feel a weird connection to Avi as she was leaving the house. She found herself anticipating their next meeting because their talk had been interesting and fun.

Chaya took one more look at the time and realized she had to head home because it was late. "Well, I should probably head home now."

Standing at the door, Avi remarked, "Of course, Chaya. Thanks again for your help tonight."

Chaya grinned, her heart warming slightly. With thanks in her voice, Chaya spoke. "I hope we can hang out again sometime."

With a smile, Avi expressed his sense of solidarity with Chaya. "Of course, Chaya. I'd love to catch up more, maybe even go for a hike together sometime."

Chaya's eyes gleamed at the idea. "That sounds wonderful, Avi. I'll definitely hold you to that offer."

Avi laughed, appreciating her zeal. "Consider it a promise, then. Now, go get some rest, and I'll see you around."

After nodding and giving a final wave, Chaya turned and left. Her mind wandered back to their talk as she drove home. She couldn't help but be pulled to Avi because of his laid-back demeanor and adventurous spirit.

Later that night, as she lay in bed, her thoughts kept returning to their exchange. She recalled how intently he listened to her tales, posing meaningful queries and passionately sharing his own experiences.

Imagined together, Chaya began to wonder what it would be like to tackle difficult hikes, discover new trails, and develop a strong friendship via their shared passion of maintaining physical fitness. A thrill of excitement ran down her spine at the prospect of spending more time with him.

She started to daydream about what it would be like to kiss

him, to feel his powerful arms enveloping her, and to disappear into the depths of his eyes.

Her fingers followed the natural curves of her body, resting longer on the areas she had stroked earlier in the evening. She couldn't help but think of Avi's reaction to her appearance when he made a statement. There was something admiring in his gaze, and she found herself drawn to him.

Chaya let herself get lost in the feelings as her fingertips glided softly over her flesh. As she drew closer to the edge of ecstasy, her heart raced and her breath quickened.

Chaya's body became more sensitive with each stroke, and her desire for relief increased. With a quiet sigh, her fingers sped up in search of the sweetest gratification.

Her desire was growing stronger by the minute, the sensation growing stronger. Chaya's body shook with excitement as she moaned at the height of her pleasure.

With her heart thumping in her chest, she closed her eyes and reveled in the aftermath of her peak.

Upon opening her eyes at last, she was still able to visualize Avi's bright blue eyes and tousled black hair. She couldn't help but wonder if her feelings for him would ever be returned.

With her skin still tingling from the intensity of her pleasure, Chaya slipped out of bed. Knowing that Avi had reawakened a part of her she didn't know existed made her grin.

Chaya could not get Avi off her mind during the course of the following few days. She used to pause every time she went by his house in the hopes of seeing him outside.

On occasion, she would even go outdoors, positioning herself carefully to catch a glimpse of him as soon as he left his home.

Chaya saw Avi's son playing with him in the yard one

afternoon when she went out for her afternoon jog. Chaya approached the group and wished Avi and his child a happy birthday. Seeing her, Avi stood up, his big form beaming.

He waved at her and said, "Hello, Chaya. Nice to see you again."

With her hands a little perspirationy, Chaya gave the motion back. "Hi,Avi. It's nice to see you too."

They had a fairly normal chat at first, talking about the weather and their individual days' activities. But Chaya couldn't help but notice how Avi's gaze followed her around while they talked. Her body began to warm, and her heart began to beat faster.

It appeared that Avi was drawn to Chaya in a similar way. The way her hair draped across her shoulders, the way her hips swayed gently—he couldn't help but observe it all. Her running attire was tight and highlighted her figure to the point that he felt like he had to focus really hard to keep his eyes off of it.

There was an unmistakable spark between them as their talk went on. Every time their eyes locked, there was an electric spark that neither of them could ignore.

Avi's thoughts were always racing, wondering what it would be like to taste her lips, feel her body against his, and actually touch her.

Chaya was thinking along the same lines. She couldn't help but observe the way Avi's hands moved with ease and confidence, and how his muscles rippled beneath his shirt. She could just picture her fingertips running along his well-defined abs and his powerful arms encircling her waist.

Avi's thoughts were always racing, wondering what it would be like to taste her lips, feel her body against his, and actually touch her.

After a couple weeks...

Just as Avi was leaving his boys for school, he heard his phone ring. When he realized it was Chaya who was phoning, he dashed to check who it was.

He said, "Hey, what's up?"

"Are you busy?" inquired Chaya. "I'm having a bit of trouble with my internet. I know it's a router issue, but the whole setup I have is way too high up for me to reach it and work on it effectively. Can you come by and fix it?"

"Yes," replied Avi. "I'll be there in about 5 minutes."

With a stepladder in hand, Avi virtually sprinted over to Chaya's residence. He knocked, and Chaya, dressed in a rather form-fitting workout attire, opened the door.

"I apologize for how I looked," Chaya remarked. "I was in middle of filming a video for my channel, and didn't have time to change"

"I don't mind at all," Avi chuckled. "It's not a bad visual at all"

Chaya turned red all the way from head to toe. She shot back, giggling a little, "Flattery will get you everywhere".

Asking, "Where is your internet setup?" Av was attempting to divert his attention from Chaya's smoldering physique.

Chaya said, "In my bedroom," and led the way upstairs. After assembling his ladder, Avi started tinkering with Chaya's router.

Chaya saw Avi from a distance, admiring his abilities and the ease with which he threaded through the tangle of cables. She was enthralled by his unwavering focus and attention to detail. Now that Avi was on a ladder, her eyes followed the contours of his strong arms and lingered on his tight ass, which was nearly precisely at eye level.

Avi talked with Chaya on a variety of subjects while he worked. Occasionally, their gazes met, and they experienced brief but powerful moments of connection—almost as if they were daring one other to go beyond friendship into something more.

After jumping off the ladder, Avi exclaimed, "All done!" As he did, he ran into Chaya, who had deliberately positioned herself far too near to the bottom step.

With the ladder providing support, he straightened and faced her. Without exchanging a word, they both understood what was about to happen when their eyes locked.

Feeling brave, Chaya grasped onto Avi's wide shoulders and drew him nearer to her. Instinctively, Avi wrapped his arms around her waist and drew her close to his body.

Their mouths touched, hesitantly at first, then more urgently. Chaya's tongue shot out, trying to find its way into Avi's lips. He welcomed with gusto, giving her permission to stick her tongue inside his mouth.

Avi's hands moved along Chaya's back, stopping at the shirt's hem. He raised it over her head quickly, letting his ravenous gaze see her nude chest. Without hesitation, Chaya mimicked his move and pulled Avi's shirt over his head, exposing themselves to each other as nude and defenseless.

A surge of heat raced through Chaya's veins at the sight of Avi's muscular, toned form. All she wanted was to feel his powerful arms encircling her and his body pressing against hers.

Avi was enthralled with Chaya's attractiveness as well. Her fit but slim physique was framed by her long, dark hair that flowed down her back. Her plump, little breasts begged to be handled and touched. The temptation was too great for him to resist.

Avi quickly dropped himself onto the bed and took Chaya with him. Their bodies matched perfectly as she straddled him. Avi's hands moved over her sides, feeling around her body's curves. Their pulse thumping frantically in their chests, their labored breathing filled the room.

With great care, Avi's hands traced every inch of Chaya's body. He came to a halt at her hips, raised her, and placed her on the bed. As she lay there, exposed and vulnerable, Chaya had a rush of exhilaration at the thought of what lied ahead.

Chaya moaned softly as Avi's hands cradled her breasts and his thumbs circled her nipples.

With an arched back, she invited Avi to explore her body even more by pressing her chest into his hands. Seeing this as a sign, Avi traced patterns on her skin with his fingers, giving her chills all over.

Chaya closed her eyes and tasted the feelings that filled her body. A chill ran down her spine as she felt Avi's lips against her neck. She let out a soft whimper as his fangs chewed on her earlobe.

She curved her back and asked him to press closer. Avi nodded, sucking and chewing on her tender flesh as he took one breast into his lips. With a quiet gasp, Chaya's hips bucking uncontrollably from the feelings pulsing through her body.

Avi's other hand reached down and touched the moisture between Chaya's legs. Gently, he opened her folds so that his fingers could touch her swelling clitoris. Chaya's body tensed with expectation, she whimpered.

Avi took his time, circling her clit and plunging within her wetness while playing with her fingers.

Under him, Chaya writhed, her body aching for more. With her hands all over his body, she grasped, tugged, scratched, and yearned for more.

Avi grinned, appreciating her zeal. He changed hands, and now he teased Chaya's clit with his other hand while playing with her other breast. Knowing exactly how to push Chaya to the verge of ecstasy, Avi applied more pressure. Her body trembled with anticipation, her breath coming in short sharp gasps.

Reaching down, Chaya touched Avi's erection, feeling the firmness and warmth of his cock. She gave him a light squeeze, signaling that she was also eager to play. Avi let out a moan and briefly stopped moving his fingers.

He saw the intensity and want burning in Chaya's eyes as he peered into them. Chaya gave him a smile that told him to keep going.

Avi smiled and went back to what he was doing with his hands. He tightened the pressure, circling her clit more quickly and forcefully while keeping a close eye on her response. Chaya's body curved towards him as her breathing grew labored, yearning for closer touch.

Chaya's fingers moved in a playful manner over Avi's

testicles, tickling and tease him. His silky hair across her palms and the silky skin beneath her fingertips were sensations she cherished. With a harder touch, she rubbed circles over his testicles, making Avi growl low in delight. She felt the power and fire radiating from his cock as she tightly held and stroked it. With a moan, Avi moved his hands more quickly and flicked his tongue across her clit.

Chaya felt the orgasm spread across her whole body like a tsunami releasing its fury. She grabbed onto Avi out of reflex, her nails going all the way into his thick back. Her screams rang out in delight, bouncing off the walls and echoing across the room.

Avi's tongue licked feverishly at her sweet nectar, without missing a beat. She rode out the waves of her climax with his muscular arms caressing her body.

Chaya's climax ended and she fell back into the bed, content and exhausted. Still hovering over her, Avi's lips kissed her inner thighs softly and murmured comforting things into her ears.

Chaya moved onto her side and faced Avi, feeling a sense of intimacy between them that had returned.

Her intense gaze conveyed a blend of curiosity and desire. Avi nodded in agreement, unable to withstand the tug of their shared attraction.

Chaya stepped toward Avi and positioned herself over his stiff phallus. Admiring its size and shape, she held it in her palm. She smiled softly, then bent forward to slowly take him into her warm, moist cavern with her mouth.

With a start, Avi rolled his eyes back in his head, too much of Chaya's lips and tongue around him. She bobbed her head deftly, forcing him deeper into her throat while he struggled to keep his grip on the sheets.

Chaya's hand followed her mouth's movements, caressing and rubbing Avi's shaft to provide yet another level of stimulation.

Her tongue moved around the tip, exerting just enough pressure to make Avi feel incredibly lustful. His veins were pumping blood at a frightening velocity as his heart raced. His breathing became more rapid and difficult.

Chaya drew Avi deeper into her lips, her tongue dancing around him in a rhythmic dance, sensing his approaching release. Pushing into her face in a primal attempt to find relief, his hips started to thrust.

Bobbing her head up and down on his shaft, Chaya matched his speed, relishing in her power over him. With every motion, Avi let out a moan as his body stiffened under the increasing strain.

The air in the room was heavy with want, the pungent smell of sweat and passion filling the air. It was as though the air itself had taken on an electrical charge, establishing an unsaid bond that went beyond simple spatial limitations.

Ever sensitive to his demands, Chaya reacted by quickening her pace and drawing him closer to her throat. Her tongue danced around him as she did so, bringing even more intensity to their private moment. Their combined experience became increasingly intense, leaving both of them gasping for air and wanting more.

Sweat and the smell of sex flooded the air, bonding them in a way that was almost physical. Sensing his imminence, Chaya picked up her tempo and pushed him more down her throat. She kept circling him with her tongue, giving him more sensation.

With his body shaking from the rush of feelings, Avi let out a cry. He unleashed his seed into Chaya's waiting mouth with one more fierce push. She took a deep breath and tasted it, relishing the full flavor.

At last, Avi's breaths slowed, and he had a satisfied, exhausted look in his eyes. He murmured, "Thank you," his voice raspy with want. Chaya grinned, her cheeks glowing with pride at having given him so great joy.

Exhausted and full, Avi let himself lean against her, their bodies entwined like a pair of parts. After his deep release, Chaya's hand continued to caress his chest, her fingers creating circles that soothed him.

"Thank you," in a hoarse voice from passion, was Avi's final words. "That was incredible."

I have to admit, that was really... intense," Chaya said, blushing a little bit. "I appreciate you sharing that with me," she said.

"I'm glad we could share this together," Avi said softly, "It means a lot to me." Their eyes met, and there was a mixture of compassion and thankfulness reflected in their depths.

Chaya was suddenly overcome with shame and added, "I'm sorry about the fact that you're still married," in a quiet voice.

With a protecting arm encircling her shoulders, Avi drew her in closer. "Don't feel sorry for me," he murmured, "because everyone has a different journey that brought them here. In any case, I'm basically divorced now; the paperwork will be finalized in a few weeks."

For a time, they laid in bed together in quiet, caressing each other and enjoying their mutual nudity. Eventually, Avi murmured, "I should get going," realizing that he had to leave because his kids would be returning home shortly.

With a trace of grief visible on her face, Chaya nodded and acknowledged that their time together was limited due to their current situation. "Yes, maybe we should stop," she said, hesitantly getting out of bed.

They got up and looked at each other, appreciating what had just happened: the connection they had made, the unfiltered feelings they had exchanged, was something neither of them had ever felt or experienced before.

After a couple weeks...

As Chaya stepped outside to greet the day, the sun cast a warm glow over the neighborhood, and she breathed in the crisp morning air, thankful for the quiet. Chaya was still getting used to living next door to Avi, a really nice man, but things had been complicated lately because of his ongoing divorce.

After spending the rest of the night chatting with his lawyer and taking care of other family things, Avi came out of his house looking exhausted but resolute. Upon seeing Chaya, a smile broke through his exhausted countenance.

We both signed last night, and I also get the kids, so it's official, he declared.

Chaya felt her heart fill with joy at seeing Avi. She was aware of his strong desire to be involved in his kids' lives.

She exclaimed, "That's amazing news!" "Your kids are lucky to have you as their dad."

As he got into his car, Avi replied, "Thank you, that means a lot." "Hope to see you around"

"It would not be missed for the world," Chaya remarked.

After returning home, Chaya ran a few errands and napped. There was a lot of noise outside that startled her.

She noticed multiple police cars parked outside Avi's house and hurried to the window to see. She concluded that something horrible had to have happened, and her heart fell.

She noticed multiple police cars parked outside Avi's house and hurried to the window to see. She quickly changed into her robe and slippers and went outdoors to look at it, perplexed.

She spotted several officers standing about Avi's house, talking animatedly among themselves, as she got closer to his front yard. Chaya, her curiosity piqued, moved to the heart of the action.

As soon as she got closer, one of the cops realized that she was Avi's neighbor. "Pardon me, ma'am," he said as he moved to speak with her. "Have you seen Mrs. Goldstein around this house today?"

Perplexed, Chaya shook her head. "No, I haven't seen her for months, and Mr. Goldstein informed me that he had gotten divorced this morning. Why do you ask?"

With a groan, the cop ran a hand through his hair. "We need to get information on her whereabouts immediately," he stated. "Seems his ex-wife showed up at the school and informed the secretary that she was picking them up. An assistant brought the boys out, and it was fifteen minutes before her superior discovered that their mom had taken them. At that point, she was long gone" said the cop. "We've been searching for her ever since. We don't know why she would take the kids, but we can't risk losing track of them again."

Chaya's emotions fell. "Oh my God, that's awful! What can I do to help? I know Avi and his kids, and I'd hate to think of them being in danger."

With gratitude, the officer gave her a look. "Any assistance you can provide would be greatly appreciated. We'll be conducting a search of the area, and if you happen to spot Mrs. Goldstein or the boy, please call us immediately."

With her thoughts buzzing with possibilities, Chaya nodded. "Of course, I'll keep an eye out and report anything suspicious."

The policeman gave his card to her. "Please don't hesitate to contact us. We'll update you on any developments."

Chaya thanked him and said she would watch out for him.

Meanwhile, a small group of police officers were gathered around the dining room table in Avi's home. Avi was listening in as Captain Julia Carter, a tough-as-nails officer with a reputation for being an expert in kidnapping cases, spoke to the task group she had put together.

"These are two very young kids who are now in potential danger. We're going to treat this case as a top priority. It's our duty to protect these children at all costs."

Julia's voice reverberated throughout the space, her resolve evident. "We'll work tirelessly to bring them back safely."

With a troubled heart, Avi nodded. "Thank you, Detective. You have no idea how much this means to me."

Julia smiled reassuringly at him. "You can count on us, Mr. Goldstein. Now, let's get moving."

Detective Carter fixed her intense gaze on the picture of Sarah Marshall that was on the screen in front of her. As Julia briefed the special task team gathered in the tiny dining room, she was aware that time was of the essence.

Julia stated, "Sarah Marshall, the ex-wife of Avi Goldstein, has abducted their two children," in a stern and determined tone. "According to witnesses, she left the school with the children and is heading towards the train station. We believe she's planning to flee across the border."

The investigators realized how serious the issue was, and the room fell silent. Julia went on, "I want every available officer on the streets, searching trains, buses, and all border checkpoints. Meanwhile, Mr. Goldstein and I will be heading to intercept her at the border, Let's move"

As soon as the group dispersed and got to work on their assignments, Chaya insisted on going with Avi and the officers to intercept Sarah and the kids since she felt just as invested in the outcome. She thought that by being there, she may provide some solace to Avi throughout this terrifying ordeal. Captain Carter jumped into her vintage Chevy Impala, and Chaya and Avi jumped into the rear seat behind her. The police car sped out of Avi's driveway and headed towards the freeway, trailing a trail of smoke from the burning tires. They passed several cars as they sped down the highway, as if they didn't realize how urgent their mission was.

Avi and Chaya held on to the seats in the automobile, preparing for the sharp bends and shocks that Captain Carter skillfully maneuvered. Chaya could hear the sirens wailing from the automobiles behind them as they raced down the freeways.

The scenery flew by as the automobile raced down the highway. Thoughts of his children, his ex-wife, and the urgent steps he had to do flashed through Avi's head. It was as if he were trapped in a nightmare from which he was unable to escape.

"You guys having fun back there?" Julia enquired, seemingly pleased by the couple's fear at her driving style.

Chaya couldn't help but feel a little bit of respect for the courageous skipper, even in the face of the dire circumstances, as he appeared completely unfazed by the thrilling voyage.

But Avi didn't lose sight of the primary goal, which was to find his sons. With his pulse thumping more quickly than the speedometer, he asked, "Any word from the cops monitoring the train stations?"

Captain Carter looked at her phone's map and nodded. "We've received updates from the officers stationed at various points. No sign of the missus yet, though"

Avi couldn't help but question Sarah's intentions as they were driving. Was she trying to get even? Or was she merely fearful for their children's safety in the midst of the chaos and foolishly trying to get them to safety? As the vehicle accelerated toward the border, these queries raced through Avi's head.

These feelings gripped Chaya as well, her heart pounding

for Avi and his sons. She didn't know what was going on, but she knew she had to stand strong for Avi. In the hopes that her supportive gesture might provide him some respite from the chaos, she reached over and grasped his hand. Thankfully, Avi seized her hand and held on to it so tightly that she could feel his fingers leaving imprints on her flesh.

At last, a voice cracked over the radio, saying, "We've got her! She's at a department store two miles away from here."

Excitedly, Captain Carter's face brightened up. "We should arrive there in ten minutes," she stated, maintaining her composure in spite of the tense atmosphere. "We'll find her soon enough."

Avi nodded, appreciative of the comfort. "Thank you, Captain."

Chaya tightened her hold on Avi's hand, offering him all the power she could summon.

The tension in the air increased as they got closer to the border. All of the people in the car appeared to be holding their breath, anticipating the moment when they would be able to see Sarah and the kids.

They reached the parking lot at last. While she concentrated on the main door, Captain Carter gave her crew orders to divide up and cover other access points.

Avi's pulse raced as they walked into the store, and he looked around him, trying to find Sarah and the kids. His eyes landed on a mother clutching a small child, the two of them looked scared and bewildered. Is that who they are?

Sarah emerged from behind a clothes rack with a frightening look on her face before he could confirm. She had a big kitchen knife in her hand; the blade gleamed in the fluorescent light.

Sarah positioned herself close to the doorway, her blade looming over the terrified youngster. The small boy's face was marked with terror, and his eyes were wide with horror.

"You allow me to leave with them and give me safe passage across the border, or they die." Sarah's voice was raspy. "I no longer care at this point"

With haste, Captain Carter and her group surrounded Sarah and the kid with a barricade. Julia spoke to Sarah in a composed manner, trying to diffuse the tension without making it worse.

Captain Carter begged, keeping her cool under pressure. "Sarah, listen to me. there's no need for violence. Let's talk about this calmly and we can find a solution for everyone involved."

But Sarah's lips curled into a menacing smile, and her eyes flashed with insanity. "No negotiations, Detective. I've already waited far too long. Today, I either get what I want or no one does"

Knowing that his sons' lives were in jeopardy made Avi's heart race with terror.

With a voice cracked with passion, Avi begged. "Please, Sarah, don't hurt them!"

Sarah's grasp on the knife tightened as her gaze focused. "They're mine, not yours," she angrily declared. "And you know what? I'm done playing nice. This is my last chance to make you understand that I won't be ignored anymore."

Chaya felt her heart tighten with terror as she saw the interaction from a distance. She recognized that her presence wouldn't be enough to stop Sarah from continuing on her terrible path, even though all she wanted was to keep Avi and his kids safe.

Captain Carter made another attempt to reason with Sarah. "Sarah, we can work together to resolve this situation. There's no need for violence."

However, Sarah just laughed uncontrollably, her enraged

eyes going crazy. "You have no idea what you've done, Avi. This is your punishment!"

Sarah swung the knife quickly in the direction of the child's neck, hate in her eyes.

However, Officer Carter leapt forward to avoid the attack and used her exceptional agility before she could make contact. Sarah lost her hold on the knife when she snatched a broken shopping cart wheel off the floor and threw it at her.

Officer Carter saw her chance and jumped at Sarah, giving her a strong karate kick to the middle of her abdomen. Sarah was thrown backward by the power of the punch, landing hard on the floor. The knife skidded a few feet off of them before coming to a stop.

With a look of intense rage in her eyes, Sarah tried to get back on her feet. She yelled, "You'll pay for this, Avi!" and lunged at Officer Carter once more.

But Captain Carter was prepared for her, and he tripped Sarah with a deft leg sweep. Julia pounced on the moment as Sarah fell to the ground, pinning her arms behind her back.

Sarah was so angry and frustrated that her body shook and sweat streamed down her face. She said, fighting against Officer Carter's hard grip, "You think you've won, but you haven't!"

Officer Carter cuffed Sarah's hands and secured them behind her back, keeping an iron hold on her to prevent her from escaping. With a composed, authoritative tone, she said, "You're under arrest, ma'am," and another officer led her into a squad car. Avi, in the meantime, went to embrace his boys and expressed gratitude that they were safe.

With her face twisted in anger, Sarah fought the restraints. She spat angrily, her words dripping with contempt, "This isn't over, Avi!"

With a solemn attitude, Captain Carter turned to face Chaya and guided her into a corner. "Listen, sweetheart, I know this isn't easy for you, but right now, Avi needs someone to lean on. He's been through hell today, and he needs a release. You're the only one who can provide that for him."

Chaya lingered, not sure how to reply. She turned to face Avi, who had agony and fatigue in his eyes. She was resolved to do everything within her ability to assist him because she knew he needed consolation.

With a quiet "Alright," Chaya moved forward. "I'll do whatever I can to help him."

But when Avi realized his kids were safe, his heart grew larger with appreciation for Captain Carter and her group. He turned to face Chaya, love and gratitude overflowing in his eyes.

Feeling the gravity of the situation, Chaya smiled gently at Avi and held out her hands. She whispered, "It's okay, Avi. We're all safe now," her touch comforting his weary spirit.

"I am aware," he said. "Let's get home" .

This time, they took a somewhat larger police van on their way home. After being startled and shocked for a while, Avi's boys quickly got enthralled with being in a police car and started pestering the driver to turn on the lights and sirens, which he gladly did. But eventually, one of them dozed off with his head on his father's lap and the other in Chaya's arms.

After the lengthy drive home, Chaya assisted Avi in putting the boys to sleep. Chaya recalled Officer Carter's note as she was leaving the room, asking that she make sure Avi was able to let go of the day's stress. She reasoned that she need to check on Avi's mental health before she went.

She followed him into his bedroom and asked, "Wanna spend some time together before I go home?"

"Yes," he said as he sat on the edge of his bed, appearing exhausted from the day's events but also carrying an unknown emotion in his eye.

Sensing his emotions, Chaya took off her shirt gently, exposing her toned, slim body. Her long brown hair cascaded over her breast as she allowed it to fall over her shoulders. Avi's gaze lingered on her body as he followed her movements.

Her dark nipples peeked with longing, her breasts tiny but well sculpted. Her navel was a perfect circle, and her stomach was toned and flat. Her hips then somewhat expanded, revealing the most alluring detail: her lace underwear just barely visible through her skirt.

With deliberate slowness, she approached him so that he

could admire her body to the fullest. She stopped inches from him, her breasts brushing his chest as she got to him. With an involuntary gasp, Avi extended his hands to clasp her waist.

With a smile, Chaya invited him to come closer by slightly separating her lips. She moved into his embrace, her breasts grazing his chest as her body pressed against his. With a gasp, Avi reached down to cup her ass and drew her in closer.

Avi had reached his breaking point. He drew Chaya closer still, his lips meeting hers in a passionate kiss. His tongue played with her lips, luring her own to gently touch his. With a gentle groan, Chaya melted into his arms and ran her hands through his hair, pleading with him to give her more.

Their tongues twisted and tangled in a lustful dance as their intense kisses grew more demanding. With a deft touch, Avi's hands moved over Chaya's curves, studying her body. His hands moved over her curves, feeling every nook and cranny of her flesh as their bodies molded together. His fingers reached down, feeling the warmth of her panty-clad crotch beneath her skirt. As his fingertips caressed her delicate skin, Chaya let out a sigh and felt her breath catch in her throat. She was aching for the release he would bring, and she wanted him so badly.

Finally giving up, Avi placed his hands on Chaya's thighs and slowly pushed her skirt up till it was gathered around her waist. Her legs were exquisitely formed, with the softness of her flesh juxtaposed against the sleek lines of her muscles.

Then he turned to her underwear, running his fingers over the sheer material and tantalizing her with the thought of what might be underneath. Chaya writhed in frustration, breathing more rapidly as she waited for him to take her back.

Chaya's body naturally arched, craving more as Avi's fingers went deeper. She was breathing quickly and sharply, concentrating all of her attention on the powerful feelings that were rushing through her body.

Sensing that she was ready, Avi slipped between her legs, his erection pulsating with passion. Taking her in his hands, he led her down his stony shaft. He stepped into Chaya, filling her to the brim with his thick length, and she gasped.

Avi moved, slamming into her with a deliberate rhythm. With a primal ferocity, Chaya's hips met his as she let out a cry, her body swaying with every movement.

Avi accelerated his tempo as his strong thrusts brought her closer and closer to the brink of ecstasy. Chaya's body trembled from the effort of keeping up with his unrelenting pace, and her breath came in short, desperate gasps.

Avi accelerated, his hands clenching her hips as he drove hard into her, desperate to let go of the stress that had built up throughout the day. Chaya's body squirmed from the amazing sensations going through her as her claws sunk into his shoulders.

Chaya could feel her climax developing inside her as their passionate kissing reached a fever pitch, a wave of ecstasy that threatened to swallow her.

With her claws pressing into Avi's back, Chaya wrapped her legs around his waist, holding on tightly. Her body trembled with anticipation as her breath came in short, quick rushes.

Avi's body shook from the strain of trying to keep control as his thrusts became more forceful. Chaya matched his zeal with her own, trying to match his passion with more desperate movements.

"I have to leave," declared Avi. "I can't get you pregnant"

Frustrated, Chaya rolled her eyes. "Look, I'm taking the medication, okay? I also have no desire to become pregnant. Just screw me, please!"

For a brief while, Avi was torn between contradictory feelings. After all he'd gone through, he knew he shouldn't be doing this with Chaya. However, he also realized that he required her and this release.

He inhaled deeply and gave in to his cravings, his hands tightening around her hips as he pushed into her once more. With a loud groan, Chaya's body welcomed his incursion.

Avi quickened his tempo, his thrusts getting harder as his desire to let go increased. Their bodies clashing created a symphony of passion that reverberated throughout the space. Chaya began to moan more loudly, her body arching off the bed in a desperate attempt to get free.

Avi kept up his fast rhythm, staring at Chaya's face as she drew closer to the brink of bliss. Chaya's cries became louder with each stroke, the force of her climax sending shivers down her spine.

Avi's body shook from trying to contain himself, knowing that his own release was fast approaching.

Finally, waves of pleasure crashed through their bodies as their simultaneous orgasms hit them like a tidal wave. As Avi's whole body trembled, his seed burst into Chaya, her body trembling from the intensity of her own release as she clung to him.

Chaya fell onto the bed, exhausted and content as the final surges of pleasure faded. With his body heaving from his own release, Avi did the same. As they lay there, their breath came in short spurts and their hearts were racing. Chaya caressed Avi's forehead with her fingers as she combed them through his hair.

He said, "Thank you," in a raspy whisper due to the intensity of their interaction.

With a smile, Chaya ran her fingers down his cheek. "You're welcome."

She bent over and gave him a soft peck on the lips. "Now, go to bed. You appear worn out."

With his eyes starting to close, Avi nodded. "Goodnight, Chaya."

"Goodnight, Avi."

Snaking his hand toward her pussy, Avi took a big breath and drew her closer, pressing his face into her neck. He whispered, "You smell amazing," in a husky, seductive voice.

As she nestled into his chest, Chaya softly teased, pulling his hand away, kissing it, and wrapping it around her. "I said goodnight, Avi," she whispered. With his eyes firmly fixed on hers, Avi nodded and said, "You can get more of me in the morning." "You're accurate. I'm grateful.

Avi drew her in closer, his arms encircling her in a protective embrace. He murmured, "You're too kind, Chaya," his voice raspy with passion. "Thank you for being here for me."

With her head pressed against his chest, Chaya listened to his heart's steady beat. Really, it's nothing. "Are we not friends?"

With a nod, Avi ran his fingers over her hair. "Yes, we are."

For some time, they remained in that state, engrossed in their own thoughts and the solace of each other's company. They eventually fell asleep together.

EPILOGUE: Avi and Chaya strolled around the park, enjoying the warm, golden glow created by the setting sun. They had spent hours strolling and conversing as they got to know one another better and exchanged tales about their families, dreams, and lives.

The aromas of nature permeated the air, including the scent of recently cut grass, blossoming flowers, and the pleasant scent of neighboring trees. The birds' nighttime melodies provided a musical backdrop for their discourse.

When they got to a bench with a view of a tiny pond, Avi leaned over to take Chaya by the waist and pulled her in close to him. For several minutes, they remained in this position, savoring each other's companionship in silence.

They eventually began their journey home. As they got to Avi's house, he urged Chaya to hold on for a moment. He dropped to one knee and took a tiny velvet box out of his pocket. A modest but classy diamond ring was found inside the package.

Chaya gazed at the ring, her eyes widening with surprise. "Avi, what is this?" she questioned, her tone filled with curiosity.

Avi said, "Chaya, my love," his voice quivering a little from emotion. As soon as I laid eyes on you, I knew you were unique. I was enthralled with everything about you— your strength, your beauty, your knowledge. And as our friendship deepened, I understood that I wanted more from you than just a friend. As your spouse, I would like to share it with you. Do you want to wed me?"

Chaya became emotional upon realizing the depth of Avi's love for her. She answered with a smile on her face, saying, "Yes, Avi. I will marry you, yes."

After Avi placed the ring on Chaya's finger, they kissed passionately and made a vow to have a wonderful life together.

Acknowledgments

The Glory of this book's success goes to God Almighty and my beautiful Family, Fans, Readers & well-wishers, Customers, and Friends for their endless support and encouragement.

About The Author

I've spent nearly a decade penning romantic novels. As a passionate writer of erotica, I craft dark, romantic erotica. Anime Naked Truth Se of Sacred Sexuality: Forbidden Seducing Short Stories of an Erotica Nude Sexy Girl Poster. Alongside Erotic Mystery Fiction, Victorian Erotica Sex, Black & African American Erotica, Euthanasia, Daddy Teaching, Forced Domination, Alpha Monster Cuckold, and BDSM for Adults, there's an Erotic Fiction in Kinky Family. I write dark, sensual romance because I adore the power of darkness and everything that it entails. Romance novels have always been my favorite kind of books, and now I'm writing them. The idea that you will like reading and enjoying my fiction as much as I enjoy pushing the frontiers of sexual pleasure in my writing thrills me more than anything else.